W9-BKV-733

WordBooks
Libros de Palabras

Food
La Comida

by Mary Berendes • illustrated by Kathleen Petelinsek

Published in the United States of America by The Child's World®
1980 Lookout Drive • Mankato, MN 56003-1705
800-599-READ • www.childsworld.com

Acknowledgments
The Child's World®: Mary Berendes, Publishing Director
The Design Lab: Kathleen Petelinsek, Design and Page Production

Language Adviser: Ariel Strichartz

Library of Congress Cataloging-in-Publication Data
Berendes, Mary.
    Food = La Comida / by Mary Berendes; illustrated by Kathleen Petelinsek.
       p. cm. — (Wordbooks = Libros de palabras)
    ISBN-13: 978-1-59296-798-8 (library bound: alk. paper)
    ISBN-10: 1-59296-798-1 (library bound)
    1. Food—Juvenile literature. 2. Cookery—Juvenile literature. 3. Vocabulary—
Juvenile literature. I. Petelinsek, Kathleen. II. Title. III. Title: Comida.
    TX355.B465 2007
    641.3—dc22   2006103382

leaf
la hoja

apple
la manzana

basket
la cesta

seed
la semilla

3

bananas
los plátanos

strawberries
las fresas

4

oranges
las naranjas

cherries
las cerezas

5

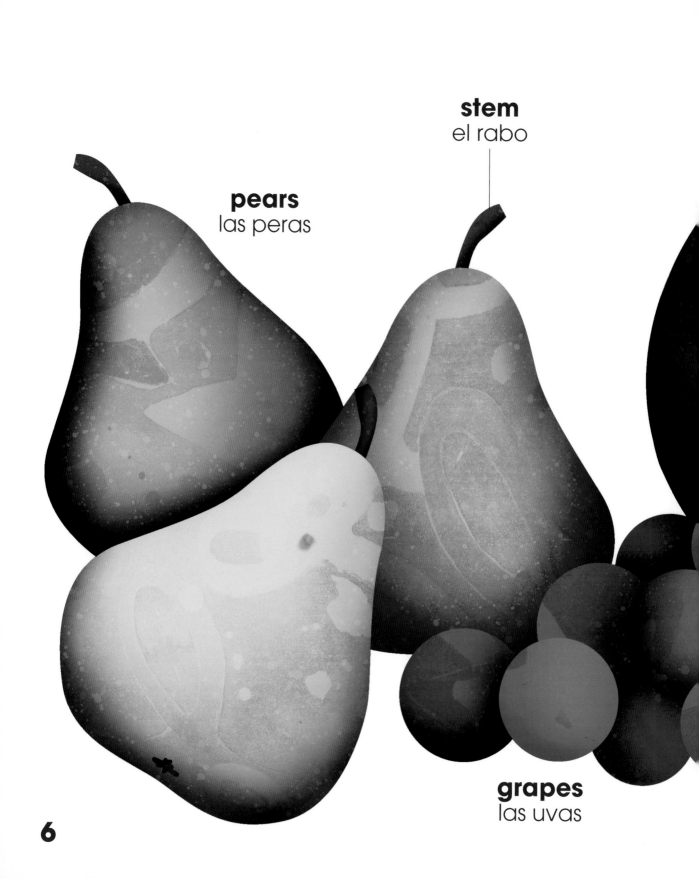

stem
el rabo

pears
las peras

grapes
las uvas

6

watermelon
la sandía

7

onions
las cebollas

corn
el maíz

8

beets
las remolachas

green beans
las judías verdes

tomatoes
los tomates

potatoes
las patatas

10

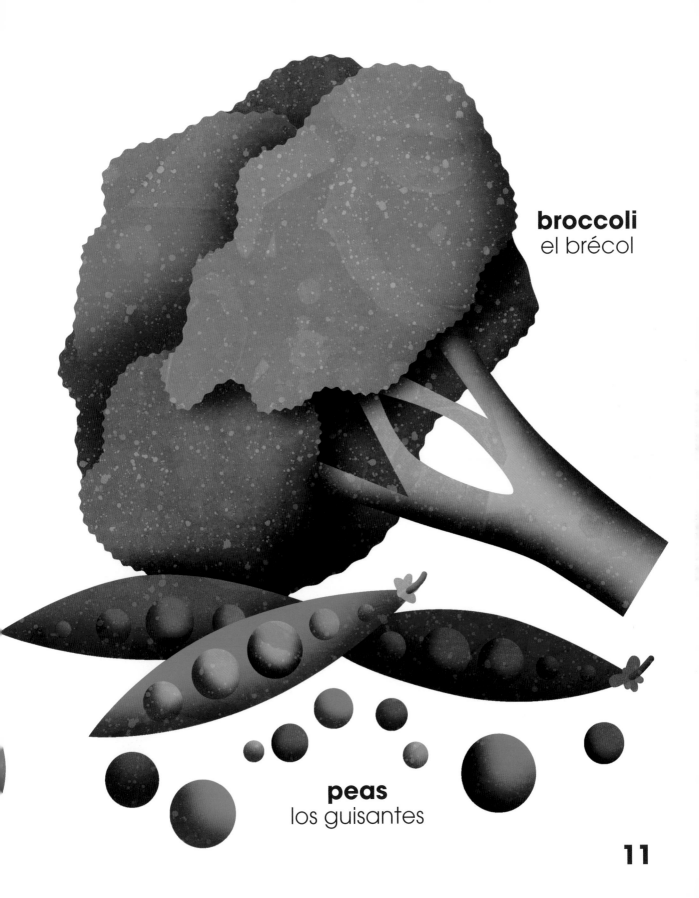

broccoli
el brécol

peas
los guisantes

11

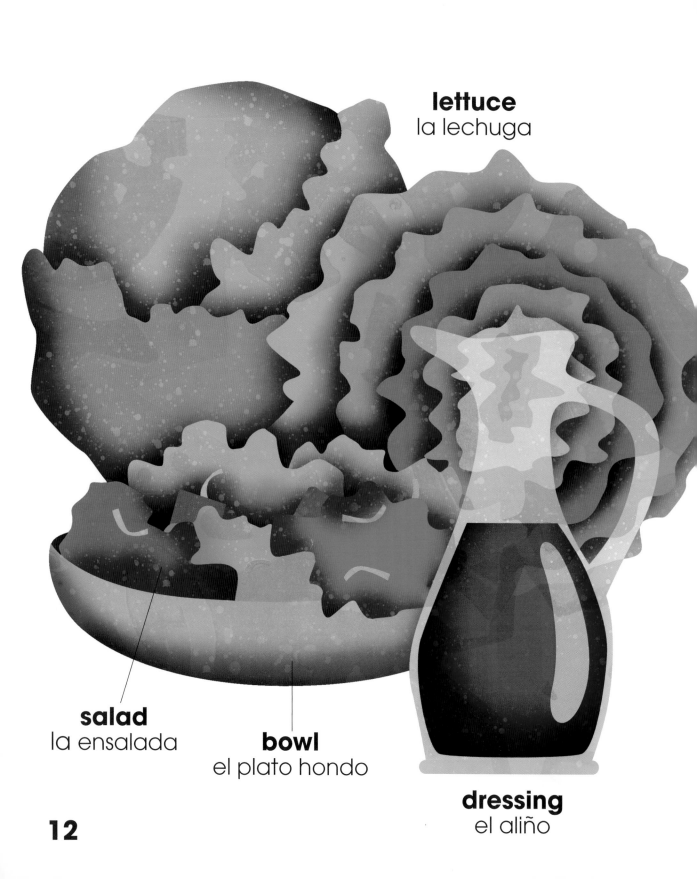

lettuce
la lechuga

salad
la ensalada

bowl
el plato hondo

dressing
el aliño

12

hamburger
la hamburguesa

bun
el panecillo

onion
la cebolla

plate
el plato

pickle
el pepinillo

13

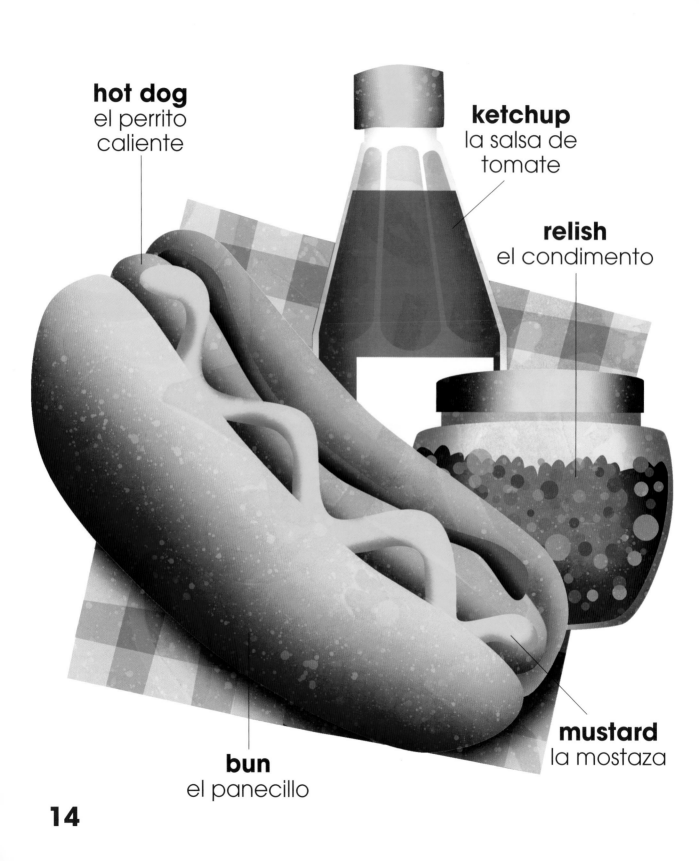

hot dog
el perrito
caliente

ketchup
la salsa de
tomate

relish
el condimento

mustard
la mostaza

bun
el panecillo

14

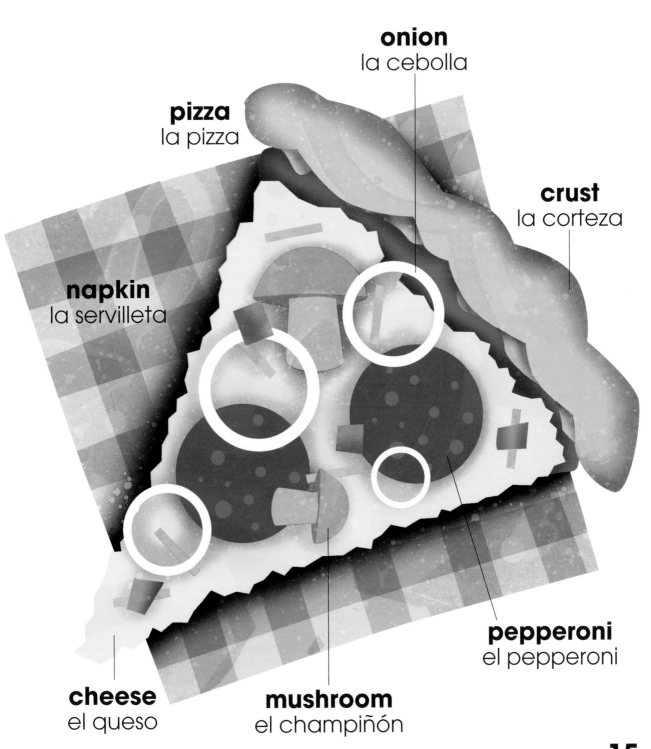

onion
la cebolla

pizza
la pizza

crust
la corteza

napkin
la servilleta

pepperoni
el pepperoni

cheese
el queso

mushroom
el champiñón

bread
el pan

butter
la mantequilla

16

spaghetti
los espaguetis

fork
el tenedor

meatball
la albóndiga

noodles
los fideos

17

glass
el vaso

milk
la leche

cereal
el cereal

spoon
la cuchara

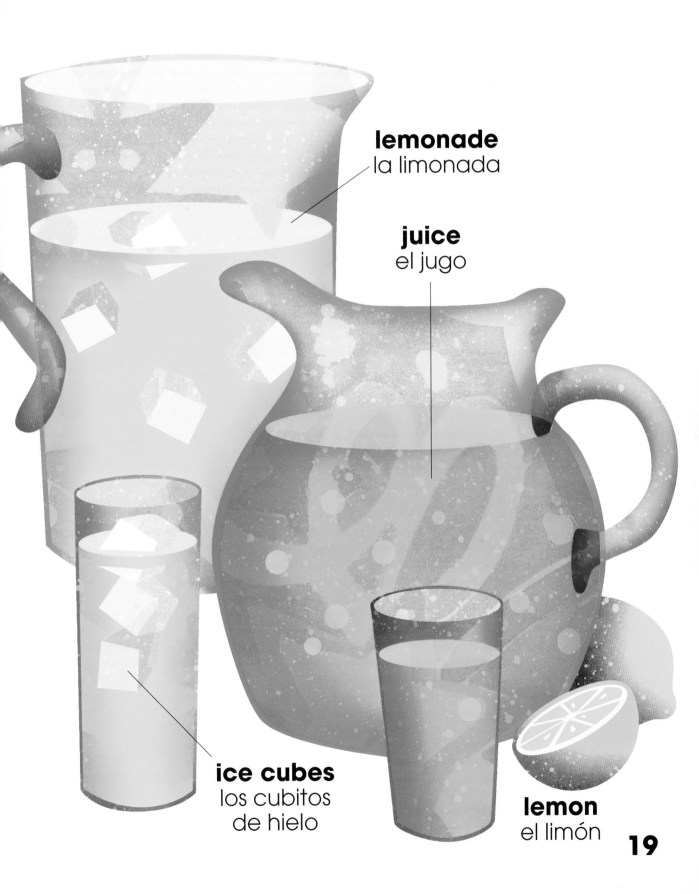

lemonade
la limonada

juice
el jugo

ice cubes
los cubitos
de hielo

lemon
el limón

19

cookies
las galletas

chocolate chips
*las chispas de
chocolate*

CHiPS

candles
las velas

cake
el pastel

slice
el trozo

pie
la tarta

blueberries
los arándanos
azules

cherry
la cereza

whipped cream
la nata montada

sprinkles
los confites

chocolate syrup
la salsa de chocolate

ice cream
el helado

23

word list
lista de palabras

English	Spanish	English	Spanish
apple	la manzana	**lemon**	el limón
bananas	los plátanos	**lemonade**	la limonada
basket	la cesta	**lettuce**	la lechuga
beets	las remolachas	**meatball**	la albóndiga
blueberries	los arándanos azules	**milk**	la leche
bowl	el plato hondo	**mushroom**	el champiñón
bread	el pan	**mustard**	la mostaza
broccoli	el brécol	**napkin**	la servilleta
bun	el panecillo	**noodles**	los fideos
butter	la mantequilla	**onions**	las cebollas
cake	el pastel	**oranges**	las naranjas
candles	las velas	**pears**	las peras
cereal	el cereal	**peas**	los guisantes
cheese	el queso	**pepperoni**	el pepperoni
cherries	las cerezas	**pickle**	el pepinillo
chocolate chips	las chispas de chocolate	**pie**	la tarta
chocolate syrup	la salsa de chocolate	**pizza**	la pizza
cookies	las galletas	**plate**	el plato
corn	el maíz	**potatoes**	las patatas
crust	la corteza	**relish**	el condimento
dressing	el aliño	**salad**	la ensalada
fork	el tenedor	**seed**	la semilla
glass	el vaso	**slice**	el trozo
grapes	las uvas	**spaghetti**	los espaguetis
green beans	las judías verdes	**spoon**	la cuchara
hamburger	la hamburguesa	**sprinkles**	los confites
hot dog	el perrito caliente	**stem**	el rabo
ice cream	el helado	**strawberries**	las fresas
ice cubes	los cubitos de hielo	**tomatoes**	los tomates
juice	el jugo	**watermelon**	la sandía
ketchup	la salsa de tomate	**whipped cream**	la nata montada
leaf	la hoja		